Mr. Bateman's Garden

Priscilla Masters

In 1842 a man called James Bateman with his wife, Maria, created a garden......

Second edition — November 1988

Copyright © P. M. Masters
Knypersley, Stoke-on-Trent.

ISBN 0 9514060 0 0

Printed by
Sherwin Rivers Ltd., Stoke-on-Trent, Staffordshire

Preface

When Gulliver Thornton and his sister, Charlotte, climb the Great Wall of China into the gardens of Biddulph Grange, they enter an enchanted world ruled by the evil ape — THOTH. Follow their adventures through an ancient tomb of Egypt, a Scottish Glen and a mystical Willow Pattern Garden. Will they and their friends find a way to free the gardens from the tyranny of Lord Thoth and his terrifying army?

But this is no ordinary army!!!

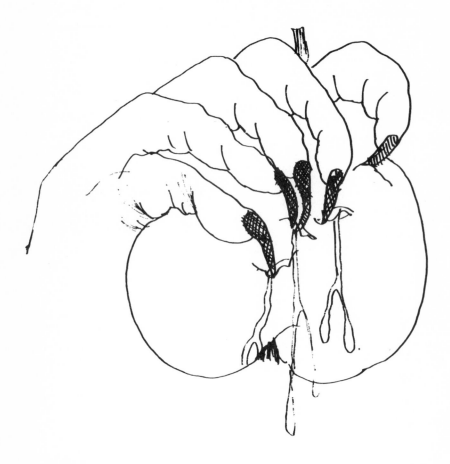

...The hand that held the apple core squeezed it so tightly the juice ran out....

CHAPTER 1

The Silent Valley

Do you know what happens to neglected gardens? I do. They go their own way. And in gardens that have gone their own way for too many years quite unpleasant things happen to the bushes and trees, to the flowers and lawns. And to the statues — yes most especially to the statues. This is a story about just such a neglected garden.

A tall thin boy was struggling to climb a wall. He was already astride but his sister, Charlie, being shorter was having problems. She couldn't reach a foothold. At last she gave up trying and leaned against the wall.

"It's no good, Gus, it's too high and my legs aren't as long as yours." She flopped down onto the grass. "I'll never make it."

The boy merely grinned. "Come on, Charlie, have another try — just once more." He peered down on the other side of the wall. "It looks great in here for a game." He leaned over as far as he dared and stretched a long arm down. "Grab hold of me and I'll pull you up... That's right," he coaxed, "put your foot down on that crack... Now HEAVE...."

The girl landed with a scrabble of loose earth beside him and together they looked into the garden.

They seemed to be at the top of a narrow, steep sided valley lined with heathers and bracken. Here and there a stone had dropped from the wall and been caught by a tangle of undergrowth. Neither of them could see the bottom — it was too dark and overgrown. Charlie looked anxiously at her brother.

"I don't want to go in."

Gus wiped the moss off his hands and onto his jeans. "Why not?"

"We shouldn't be here."

He turned and looked at her. "Who's going to bother? It's only an old garden. No one cares about it. Why should they mind that we're in here. We won't do any harm."

"It must belong to someone, Gus." She looked anxiously around her, "It's trespass. It gives me a creepy sort of feeling."

Gus laughed. "You and your imagination...."

"Don't laugh," she begged, "It feels as though...."

"Yes?" the boy said scornfully.

"... as though.. if I turned around very quickly I'd see someone spying on us."

"Rubbish."

. . . .

1

It happened that Charlie was right and Gus was wrong. Not very far away was a yawning black hole which led into a slimy black tunnel with walls that dripped. At the end of this tunnel sat a fat ugly creature gnawing an apple core.

He looked up as soft footsteps approached. "Yes?" he snarled, "what do you want?"

"Intruders are entering the garden, Sire, if it please your Great, Gruesome Majesty."

The creature's eyes glowed like two red-hot coals and the hand that held the apple core squeezed it so tightly the juice ran out and dribbled down to his fat, black, hairy belly. "No it doesn't please me, Captain Needle," he snarled. "We don't want intruders here. I shouldn't have to remind you of that. Get rid of them."

Captain Needle bowed so low his top scraped the floor of the cave. "Yes, Great Gruesome Majesty," he whined.

The Creature looked up. "What sort of intruders are they, anyway?"

"I think, Great Gruesome Majesty, that they are what are commonly called Children."

"Children?", the Creature bellowed, "Did you say Children?" And he paused for a moment and stroked his fat triple chin. "I wonder," he muttered, "I wonder."

"Keep your eye on them, Needle," he said, "sneak up on the nasty Children. Find out what they're up to. And then report back to me. Be sly, Needle, be cunning. Or I'll chop your top off."

When the soft, shuffling footsteps had disappeared back down the tunnel, the Creature gnawed his apple core until he gnawed so hard he bit his finger. "Bah!" He snarled.

. . . .

Gus and Charlie sat for a while looking around them. It was quiet — too quiet. Not a bird sang — not a leaf stirred on the trees. Even the little silver stream at the bottom of the valley rippled over the stones without so much as a splash. The whole valley was silent as though it was waiting for something — or someone.

"I think it would be better," Charlie said nervously, "if we played Hide and Seek somewhere else."

"No." Gus was in one of his stubborn moods.

He jumped down. "You can do the counting and I'll hide."

She hesitated.

"I said," he repeated, "you can start counting. I'll hide."

"All right."

She jumped down too and buried her head against her arms. Then she began to count. "One, two, three, four..." and so on.

For a minute Gus simply looked around for really good hiding places where his sister would never find him. His eyes landed on a tree — a great huge oak with an ideal split in the trunk. He ran down the side of the valley and turned left when he reached the path. He pulled himself up by the overhanging branch and curled himself up in a tiny ball. He giggled. She would never find him.

Then he heard the Peculiar Noise. It was a strange sound, a deep, rasping noise as though someone was filling their lungs with a breath of air, sucking it in. It wasn't Charlie — he could still hear her at the top of the bank, counting. But if it wasn't her it must be someone else. The problem was this. Should he crouch further down so they didn't see him? Or should he have a peep? He decided to have a peep.

He peered over the trunk right along the whole of the path. But he couldn't see anyone. And infuriatingly the noise got louder until he identified it. Someone, in this garden, was playing the bagpipes. A hoarse, whispery voice bellowed out *'Scotland The Brave.'* and then broke off to speak.

"Now where's that Wee Laddie gone to?"

Gus pressed down into the hollow trunk enormously anxious not to be found.

The hoarse voice spoke again. "He canna be verra far awee. I really oughta be warnin' him." The voice sighed and the footsteps crunched away up the path. Slowly Gus raised his head and peered through the knot in the bark. But the Piper had disappeared. All he saw was an empty path stretching along the bottom of the valley until it turned left over a stone bridge that crossed a stream.

"Ninety eight... ninety nine... a hundred. Ready or not, " sang Charlie, "I'm co-o-o-ming."

He heard her slither down the bank and smothered a giggle as he peered through the knot in the wood to see her dodging in and out of the trees, cautiously — as though she expected him to dart out. At the bottom she stood still, a finger on her chin, wondering which way to turn. He giggled again as she started the wrong way — towards the path which led to the stone bridge. Gus shifted a bit. This crack in the tree was too cramped for his long legs. He stretched them out and risked another peep — and nearly fell out of the tree with shock.

Behind Charlie, hopping jerkily from side to side was a huge, bright green frog. And Charlie was skipping gaily along without the least idea that anything was behind her.

He stood up and waved his arms. "Charlie," he shouted, "behind you. Look behind you." She wheeled around quickly — but not quite quickly enough for the frog. He had whipped behind a nearby stone, out of sight.

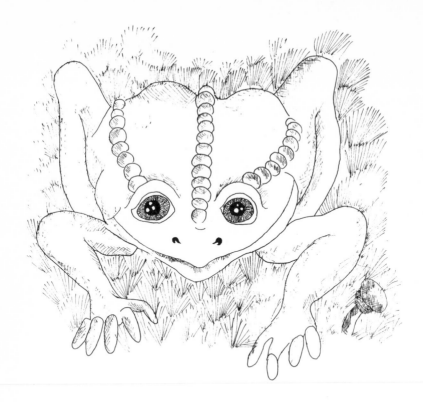

"My name is Bracken and I live here in Mr. Bateman's Garden."

"You are silly," the girl grumbled, "why did you go and give the game away? You've spoilt it now. I would have taken ages to find you in such a brilliant hiding place."

Gus jumped down from the tree and ran towards her. "Didn't you hear someone hopping behind you?"

She shook her long fair hair. "No."

"Well didn't you hear the bagpipes?"

"I heard something," she said, puzzled, "but I didn't know what it was."

Gus stared around him, suddenly feeling strange. "There's something funny about this place," he said slowly, "first the bagpipes, then the frog...."

"What frog?"

"There was a big green frog hopping behind you on the path."

"Oh yes?" she said, disbelievingly.

"Yes," he said, "there was." He walked over to the moss covered boulder. "Now do you believe me?"

Charlie stared. "Goodness," she said, "a statue."

The frog blinked up at them with two bulging yellow eyes then he gave a slow, ugly smile. "Actually," he said gulping nervously, "I'm not a statue. I'm a real frog — or I was until someone turned me into stone. My name," he said, bowing, "is Bracken and I live here in Mr. Bateman's Garden."

CHAPTER 2

Bracken

They stared at the frog and the frog stared back. Then Gus frowned.

"I've never heard a frog talk before."

The frog gave another of his wide, ugly smiles. "I know out there," He waved his hand vaguely towards the wall, "that frogs can't talk, but in here things are quite different."

He hopped right over the boulder and held out his arm. "Goodness — I was almost forgetting my manners. Welcome to Mr. Bateman's Garden. By the way — how did you get in?"

"We climbed over the wall."

"Oh," said the frog, "wasn't that a little dangerous?"

"Dangerous?" Charlie looked alarmed.

"You may have been noticed."

Gus smiled. "We didn't see anyone. We kept a careful lookout."

"They can be very cunning," said the frog, peering around with his yellow eyes.

"Who can be cunning?"

"The trees," whispered the frog.

"I'm not frightened of trees." Gus began to laugh but the frog stopped him. "You would of these trees." And he gulped again.

"We did hear some bagpipes."

"Oh you don't need to worry about him. He's a friend."

"Who?" they said together. "We didn't see anybody."

The frog looked sad. "Nobody has for sixty years."

Charlie scratched her head. She was feeling confused.

"I suppose I'd better explain," said the frog patting a cushion of soft green moss. "Why don't you sit down?"

He settled down opposite them, staring hard with his bulging yellow eyes and gulping nervously. "The Gardens that you are in," he began in his croaking voice, "were planted over a hundred years ago by a man called Mr. James Bateman with his wife, Maria. I suppose," he said thoughtfully, "that you could call them our 'Creators'. Their love for the Gardens made them a special sort of place. Inside the flowers bloomed more brightly than outside — and

5

they smelled more sweetly too. The trees grew taller here, it was said, and straighter and the bulbs multiplied faster, so fast that in spring the banks were simply smothered in bright carpets of Daffodils and Narcissi, Crocuses and Snowdrops. They created different countries too, Italy, Scotland, Egypt and China. Around the Gardens they built a Great Wall, called the Great Wall of China. And it kept the magic in.''

"My mother taught me to speak Human English."

6

"By the way," he added gravely, "I rather think it was over this wall that you two must have entered."

Gus and Charlie shifted uncomfortably.

"While we remained inside these Great Walls, we were all quite and absolutely one hundred per cent safe. We could walk and talk and hold on to the powers that had been given us. But one day..." His eyes grew sad, "... our two beloved Creators were forced to leave and the Gardens were watched over by another family. Sixty years ago they too left. Since then we have been sieged in the Sixty Years War."

"You see stones fell from the Wall. Through the breach Evil seeped in and our Good Magic leaked out. We were no longer safe from the influence of the Beneath World. Things entered through the holes where the stones had dropped out — and all of them bad — greed and the love of power over weaker beings, cruelty and spite. All the Dark Forces from which Mr. Bateman's beloved garden had been protected. Worst of all," he ended dismally, "within the dark tomb of Egypt Evil found a willing subject and in him it began to concentrate." The two children shivered and the frog glanced first over the one shoulder then the other. "His name is Thoth. With each stone that fell from the wall more and more Evil seeped in and Thoth gathered around him an army of Pine trees, magically able to walk on roots that served as feet. They developed one eye in the centre of their trunk and a mouth to speak."

"What's he like? — this Thoth."

"Nobody ever sees him," whispered Bracken. "He stays deep inside his Tomb. It was he who changed me into stone one day when I ventured near the entrance. He wants to be Lord of the Garden and none of us dares defy him."

"I wouldn't let him boss me about."

"You would if you saw him," said Bracken.

Charlie stared hard. "What's so awful about him?"

"He's ugly. Just to prove how ugly, look at me.

"I used to be a real frog. I used to hop around the gardens keeping the fly population down. And for relaxation I used to swim in the Bottomless Lake. Look at me now," he added sadly. "Stone. If I stand still for long enough everyone, even my best friends, thinks I'm a statue. The birds perch on my head and drop their whatsits down my face. If I tried to swim in the Bottomless Lake I would sink to the Beneath World and there would be no way back.

"Macduff refused to bow to Him too and just look what he did to him? Nobody's even seen him for sixty years. Thoth made him invisible. That's how strong his rotten magic is."

"Yes — but what exactly is this — Thoth?"

7

Bracken leaned in so close they could hear the big red watch ticking quietly on his chest. "That's the worst of it," he said, "We don't actually know."

"Didn't you see him when he turned you to stone?"

"I did," said the frog, "but I forgot it again. It was too terrible for my mind to keep it in so it threw it out."

(Down by the stream, two tall Pine trees stood still like sentinels. They swayed in the breeze and shifted their weight from root to root. Standing still for too long made them feel like ordinary trees. And that they were not.)

Gus, Charlie and Bracken looked at one another. Gus spoke first. "I really think," he said, "that you lot in here need help."

Charlie nodded in agreement. "So do I." The frog grinned up at them. "I was rather hoping you'd feel like that."

They were distracted by a low grumble from beneath the ground, as though they were sitting over a volcano that was wondering whether to erupt or go back to sleep.

Charlie leapt up, alarmed. "What's that?"

"It's all right," said Bracken, gently patting the ground. "It's only the bulbs. You see — Thoth won't let them come up and the Snowdrops are long overdue. It's practically time for the Crocuses and Daffodils."

"What about Spring then?"

"Some say," said the frog, shaking his enormous head sadly, "some say it might not come to the Garden at all this year. Thoth's magic is too strong."

"I can't think of anything worse than no spring," said Charlie.

Bracken carried on, gloomily. "Last year not one summer bird came. They all flew to safer places. You see, to punish them the year before, Thoth sent Spiteful Frost in the middle of June. Some of the young died in their nests." He looked hard at them. "Didn't you notice how quiet it is here? Nothing sings now in Mr. Bateman's Garden. This valley is quite, quite silent."

Gus looked around him. "There must be something you can do," he said angrily, "You can't simply stand by and let such lovely gardens die."

The frog looked even sadder. "We've tried all sorts of things to beat him and his wooden army — but they're everywhere, spying on us all the time, listening to every word we say, creeping up when we least expect it, watching us with that one eye they have in their trunks."

(Down the bank the two trees gave a low chuckle and winked at one another.)

"If we do anything at all that might annoy Him they threaten to arrest us and take us to see Him, inside that horrid black tomb." His mouth drooped. "And that's enough to make even the bravest person a bit of a coward." He gave a great, noisy gulp. "And I'm not even brave at all. I'm no hero. I just want to be a real frog again so I can go for a swim in the lake."

The rumbling began again, but this time twice as loud as the last. "They want to come up," said Bracken unhappily. "Nature is sending them upwards to the sun. It's been a long winter sleeping in the soil beneath the frost and snow. The ground is warming, the nights are getting lighter. They sense it. They know it's time. They want to see the yellow sunshine for themselves but he won't let them." He banged the ground with his small fist. "I hate Thoth." he shouted. (The two tall trees slipped away.)

"How can he stop them," asked Gus curiously. "What does he do?"

"He musters all the Pines together," said the frog," then he orders them to march." He frowned angrily. "They stamp on the little green shoots with their ugly pale feet."

The rumbling continued, sadly now and a little quieter.

Charlie spoke. "I've never heard bulbs rumble to be let out before."

Bracken stared. "Haven't you?"

"Neither have I," said Gus.

"Well if you'll pardon me saying so," said the frog, frowning, "you obviously haven't been listening hard enough." He sighed. "But then my mother did tell me that very few humans do. They never listen to plants and animals. I suppose," he said thoughtfully, "that they're far too busy talking amongst themselves to listen to what we've got to say. I think that They think we're dumb — and stupid. But of course it isn't that. We simply talk a lot quieter. And then we do have our own language."

"What?" they said together.

The frog stared. "Don't tell me you don't even know. What on earth do they teach you in schools these days?"

"History and Maths, English....." began Gus.

"You're speaking our language," pointed out Charlie.

"Ah yes," said Bracken modestly, "but my mother was a very educated and far sighted frog. She taught me to speak Human English. Of course," he added hastily, "I don't speak Human Chinese or Human Russian or..."

"Human English," said Charlie, "what other sorts of English are there?"

"Oh," said the frog airily, "absolutely hundreds. I mean to say there's Good Frog English for a start — then there's Traditional Olde Oake English, Gorse Gossip or Grass Gabble, Tree Twitter, Bluebell English (A most difficult language to follow. I don't advise beginners

9

like you to even attempt to learn it. Bulb Babble is much easier and most Bluebells speak at least a spattering of it.)''

Gus stared disbelievingly. "Say something in Bulb Babble then." The frog opened his huge mouth and gave a series of high pitched hums followed by a loud gulp. They both stared. "Golly".

Bracken looked pleased. "Quite a poetic and musical language, isn't it?''

"Er... Yes." They both stared, until Charlie caught sight of something scuttling up the path. It took a while for them to decide what it was. At first they thought it was a small, brown person. It was only as the thing drew nearer that they realized it was a small bush, with a thick tangle of twigs over skinny green legs. It waved thin branches in the air. Two dark eyes rested on them and the bush scuttled up the bank, towards them. "Bracken, thank goodness I've found you," she gasped. "I didn't know where you were, I've been hunting for you all over the garden and I couldn't find you anywhere and ...."

"Calm down, Bilberry and get your breath back. Then you can tell me what the matter is."

The bush opened her eyes very wide. "It's the Pines," she panted "Captain Needle and the rest of the Pines. They said you were sheltering intruders. They're searching everywhere for you. They said they would arrest you and take you to ... HIM." She flung two thin branches around the frog's squat neck. "Don't let them find you, Bracken, please."

He looked kindly down at the small bush. "Don't worry," he said again. "We can hide in the cave. They can't get there. They're too tall to fit in. We'll all be perfectly safe."

He turned to the children. "You'd better come with me," he said, and they all scrambled down the slope.

He led them towards a stone archway then turned sharp right to a narrow cleft in the rock. One by one they squeezed in, pushing further along in the dark until the cleft opened out into a dark cave lit only by the narrow shaft of light that beamed in through the tiny entrance. They were squashed like sardines in a tin — but they were safe — for now. Huddled together they listened.

At first they heard nothing but the deathly stillness in the Garden, then it became the gentle whisper of a breeze, shaking the leaves — no more than a twig or two snapping underfoot, a few birds taking to the air. Then they heard a quiet, soft noise. It was a horrid noise — a slug leaving its slimey trail along a path, the sly sneak of a snake crawling along on its soft white belly, the soft paw of a great dog padding nearer... nearer... dragging, slow footsteps.

Bracken shrank back into the cave. "It's Them," he whispered. "They're coming."

Charlie jumped as a harsh, rasping voice spoke not too far away. "I don't see anyone here."

Another voice replied in a higher, whining tone. "But they **were** here a minute ago; we saw them ourselves, talking to the frog."

The third voice to speak was low and full of spite. "We should find them and present them to our Great Gruesome Majesty, Thoth."

And the first voice answered. "I know that, Dimwit. But first we have to find them."

"That frog should be punished," spoke a fourth. "If he shelters intruders he should take the consequences."

"Yes," said another, "We don't want intruders here."

"And no traitors either."

"Thoth Rules," a few shouted at once.

"My roots and twigs," squeaked Bilberry. "Sometimes that Thoth — I could kill him myself."

"My roots and twigs," squeaked Bilberry.

"Sssh," they said together, "they'll hear you."

"Sorry."

From outside the leader's voice cut in, "let us report back to our Master."

The footsteps dragged away slowly and Gus ran to the front of the cave and risked a peep. Four huge Pine trees were swaying along the path on broad white feet. He shivered. There was something unpleasant about those slimey, slug-like feet that belonged underground. He would not like to meet their owners face to face. He turned back into the cave and spoke to Charlie. "It's starting to get dark," he said uneasily, "we ought to go home. What time is it Bracken?"

The frog picked up a huge red watch that dangled around his neck on a gold chain. "What time would you like it to be?"

Gus stared. "Watches don't show what time you would like it to be," he said, "They show what time it is."

The frog laughed. "Not this one," he said. "I never thought it fair that watches should obey Time. And this one never has. Time obeys it."

Gus scratched his head. "Six o'clock?" he asked tentatively.

Bracken moved the small winding button on the side and the big hand moved around slowly to the o'clock and the small hand to six. The watch gave a quiet 'Ping' six times and Bracken nodded. "Six o'clock," he announced. Then he suddenly looked forlorn. "You will come back. won't you?"

Charlie slipped an arm around him. "Of course — as soon as we get up in the morning."

"Promise?"

"We promise."

Bracken hopped outside to check whether the path was clear and it was safe for them all to leave the cave and then he and Bilberry walked back up the bank with them towards the gap in the Great Wall. Bilberry and Bracken stood and waved until the two children had jumped down the Other Side of the wall and had disappeared out of sight. "I like them, Bracken," the bush said thoughtfully, " I like them a lot — but don't you think we should have told them that bit about Human Blood?"

The frog blinked and stuck out his tongue thoughtfully, much to the annoyance of a passing Horse Fly who ended up being digested.

"I don't think so, Bilberry," he said when he had gulped the Horse Fly down. "You see they probably wouldn't have come back again, would they?"

"I still think they ought to at least know," she said doubtfully, "they would have been more... careful."

Bracken's bulging yellow eyes rested kindly on the bush.

"Bilberry," he said seriously, "they're our only chance. Without them we may as well surrender right now. When they come tomorrow, we'll introduce them to Macduff. Together we must work out a plan."

The bush nodded doubtfully.

CHAPTER 3

Mr. Thornton's Incredibly Tasty Meat Pies

It wasn't very far to their home, up the road, past the Post Office, around the corner and they were there. Their house had a small lawn in the front around which grew assorted flowers and weeds. And the front door was painted bright yellow with a lot of cat scratches near the bottom. They walked past the front door around to the back and pushed it open.

Just before Gus pushed open the door, he turned to his sister. "I don't think we'd better tell exactly what we've been doing," he said cautiously "It might cause..."

"Problems," put in Charlie.

"They'd think we were making the whole thing up anyway. So......"

"Not a word."

"I wonder what's for tea. I'm starving." They grinned at each other. They both knew what wouldn't be for tea.

Their father, Mr. H. R. Thornton owned a factory which manufactured meat pies. It made all sorts of varieties: Chicken and Mushroom, Steak and Kidney, Steak and Ale, Meat and Potato and Just Steak. They were marketed by an Extremely Efficient Sales Representative called Grits under the encouraging name of MR. THORNTON'S INCREDIBLY TASTY MEAT PIES. They supplied all the Fish and Chip shops for an eighty mile radius and everyone agreed they were — Incredibly Tasty. However, as their father spent his entire working life surrounded by meat pies of various shapes, sizes and flavours the last thing he liked to have for tea when he came home was meat pies (even if they were Incredibly Tasty). The result was that they were strictly banned from the Thornton's house.

"Hello, Mum."

She glanced up at the kitchen clock shaped like a bright red frying pan. It read five minutes past six. "Well done," she said approvingly, "you're actually on time — for once."

13

Charlie nudged Gus. "It worked."

Their Mum turned back to the stove. "Wash your hands," she said, "and sit down. Tea will be ready in a minute."

Mr. H. R. Thornton walked in through the door and they all stared at him. Charlie spoke first.

"What's the matter, Dad?"

His mouth drooped, his shoulders drooped — even his moustache drooped. Bravely he tried to smile — but that drooped too.

Their Mum bustled in, "have a cup of tea, dear," she said kindly.

"Blasted machine broke down," he said at last. "Had to fill five hundred Meat and Potato Pies all by hand."

He looked even more droopy. "I shall have nightmares all night about meat pies chasing me around the factory. Sometimes I wish I'd gone in for Liquorice Allsorts — or Jelly Babies — at least something else."

Mrs. Thornton tried to put a brave light on it. "Can't you get it mended, dear?"

H. R. Thornton groaned — loudly. "Chap's coming round first thing in the morning. It's Chicken and Mushroom day tomorrow. Have to get in early."

"Wake us up early too."

Charlie looked over at Gus.

Her father grinned at her. "What Deadly Deeds are you planning for the morning, little chicken?" he asked, smiling.

"Secrets," she said and gave an enigmatic smile.

They all watched television that night until late and around nine o'clock Gus and Charlie began to yawn.

"Bed, you two — and don't think you'll be able to stay up late when you're back at school."

They left their Dad gently snoring underneath the newspaper. Charlie glanced down at him. "I think it's Dad who needs bed," she giggled. Their last words to each other that night were "First thing in the morning."

. . . .

Bracken was crouching beneath the Wall as they climbed over into the Silent Valley. His yellow eyes gleamed as he saw them.

"I was a bit afraid you wouldn't come."

"We don't desert friends."

Bracken gave one of his wide, ugly grins and blushed bright pink. It clashed most horribly with his green skin.

"A-hem." A flattened patch of ground nearby appeared to shift and clear its throat.

14

"Oh, I nearly forgot," Bracken said, confused, "this is Macduff." In front of their eyes the flat patch of grass sprung up and two deep footprints appeared right in front of them.

Bracken spoke — it seemed to the empty air. "These are the two children who might be able to help us," he said. "Their names are Gus and Charlie."

To Gus's enormous shock he felt his hand being grasped firmly and pumped up and down. "How do you do?" said a deep voice. "Ma name is Macduff. I'm terrible glad to be meetin' you." Gus was too amazed to say a single word.

Next it was Charlotte's turn to have her hand grabbed and pumped up and down by the empty air and the voice spoke severely. "I do wish, Bracken, that you wouldna keep forgettin' ma verra existence."

Bracken blinked and looked ashamed. "Sorry — but you are rather easy to forget, umm being invisible and all that."

"Would you mind not rubbin' it in," said the voice crossly. "It's bad enough not bein' able to see you ain feet without your best friends makin' mention of it whenever they can."

"You know what, you two, it's sixty years now since I had so much as a sightin' of ma ain two feet and my wee bagpipes."

"Really?" Gus said politely.

"Look," Bracken said hastily, "we didn't meet here just to talk about your feet. We're supposed to be Thinking."

"Noo," said Macduff doubtfully, "although ma feet, if you'll pardon me makin' mention of them again, ma feet do have a bearin' on our conversation. But you're right. What we need is a Plan. And if you don't mind me bein' a wee bit pessimistic, it'll have to be a darned good one."

Bilberry scratched her head and a loose twig fell out. "Let's hide in the Watch Tower," she said. "We can keep a better look out from there. We'll have warning if anyone is around."

"Very sensible," Bracken said approvingly.

They made their way along the path which wound its way through the deep Scottish Glen. As they rounded the corner and spotted the Watch Tower looming tall and grey ahead of them they heard the sound of chanting and the slap of soft roots marching along the path behind them.

*"Left Root
Right Root
Quick March Trees.*

*Left Root
Right Root
Quick march ...."*

15

"Quickly in here." Bracken pushed open the door in the base of the tower and they all scrambled inside.

Bracken spoke. "They seem a bit more business-like today."

"To my mind." said a voice right behind them, "they have the sound of an army preparing to go into battle."

"That's what I thought," squeaked Bilberry. "Do you think...." Her voice faded away.

"I wouldn't be surprised if it's us they're after. There aren't too many of us left — only a few, waiting to be driven out."

"Worse still to toe the line to him".

"I don't think we stand much chance, if you want my opinion."

Bracken hopped sharply into the middle of the floor. "Don't say that," he begged, "where there's life there's hope."

"We may as well give up now man."

"Yes," agreed Bracken miserably.

"Mind ye I'd rather die in battle with ma claymore in ma hand than be remembered as a yellow coward. But we always run the risk of human blood touchin' Him."

Bracken's mouth drooped lower. "What chance have we got? Thoth with all his powers and his army of Pines, his magic. It's hopeless."

"Don't say that, Bracken." Bilberry scuttled across the floor and sat next to the frog. "Nothing's ever hopeless."

"Look," Gus pointed out sensibly, "all this is getting us nowhere, getting down in the dumps about it. Let's think."

They all sat quietly and thought — and thought.

Until something struck Charlotte that had been said before.

"What was that you said about human blood?"

"Oh, dear!" Bracken looked uncomfortable. "Oh my Goodness — Oh my bulging yellow eyes." He leaned closer. "I'm afraid that the legends say that if Thoth is touched by just one drop of Human Blood, he becomes immortal."

"Immortal!"

"Lives for ever and ever," confirmed Bracken looking more and more miserable.

"Oh no!" Charlie stared at the floor, "I had the feeling it would be something like that."

Bilberry sidled up to the girl. "Don't worry," she said, "we won't let him anywhere near you."

Charlie tried to smile. "I can't see how you would be able to stop him."

"Exactly." Bracken flicked out his tongue angrily. "How can we? An invisible Piper, a bush who runs away from her own shadow, a stone frog who sinks if he tries to go for a swim? What chance have we got?"

16

"Think. Don't panic," said Charlotte.

"Let me play ma wee bagpipes a while. It helps me to think."

Bilberry scratched the top of her head with a twig arm.

Bracken sat and gulped nervously.

The bagpipes struck up a wailing tune.

Gus and Charlie shut their eyes in concentration.

None of them could think of a thing.

"Food helps me think."

Bracken held out his watch.

"What Time's lunch at your house?"

"One."

He twirled the hands of his watch until the small hand was on the one and the large hand on the twelve. "Done," he said.

"We'll come straight back afterwards."

CHAPTER 4

Arrested

Lunch was just being put out on the table as they walked in through the front door. They ate so fast their mother warned them they would get indigestion.

"Slow down, you two," she laughed. "What's the big hurry?"

"Secrets."

Less than twenty minutes later they were once again scrambling over the Great Wall of China, refuelled for the afternoon — although they still couldn't think of a plan to beat Thoth for once and for all.

They dropped over to the other side half expecting either Bracken or Bilberry to be waiting — but no one was there. The Silent Valley was waiting.

"I wonder where they are."

"Still in the Watch Tower," Gus suggested, "thinking up a plan." They slithered right to the bottom of the bank and ran along the gravel path towards the stone archway until they came to the Watch Tower looming over them, grey castle ramparts tall against the sky. But a shock was waiting for them. The door swung ominously open, banging emptily in the wind to and fro. Charlie had a nasty feeling about the way the door swung so wide — like a hungry mouth. She shivered and hung back.

"Come on." Gus grabbed her hand.

They stepped inside and shouted up the stairs. "Bracken, Bilberry, Macduff — are you up there?"

17

There was no answer. They called again.

"Bracken, Bilberry, Macduff — are you there?"

Their voices echoed along the walls but there was still no answer.

"We'd better go up."

They twisted round the stairs very slowly, more and more afraid of what was waiting for them at the top as they drew nearer the trap door which led into the Tower Room. But when their heads at last peered into the square room, they saw. It was empty. Their friends had gone.

"Oh... No." They looked at each other, afraid of the worst.

"Look." Charlie ran into the centre of the room and picked up a small twig. "I'm sure this is Bilberry's hair."

"And this." Gus picked up a piece of torn ribbon. "This is hers too." He ran his finger along the frayed end. "It looks as though there was a bit of a struggle."

"Gus — look — over there." Charlie pointed to a corner where rain had formed a shallow puddle. Around were the footprints of a frog. Worse — all around were the dragging marks of tree roots. They looked hopelessly at one another. "The trees have been." It was all they said. There was no need to say another word. They could imagine it all too well — the soft roots slapping round the corners of the stairs, the tall tops peeping into the room, the struggle and the fight, Bilberry's torn twigs and ribbon, her terror and then their friends being marched away — to Thoth?

Gus sank down on the stone seat. "We shouldn't have gone for lunch," he said. "We should have stayed. We should have stayed here, with them."

"Don't be silly," Charlotte pointed out. "If we'd been here too, we'd simply have been dragged off with the rest of them."

She sighed and crossed the room, tripping over something as she did so — something soft that let out a mournful wail as she touched it. She stooped and felt it — a bag with long things sticking out of it. It took her a minute or two to work out what it was.

"Bagpipes," she whispered. "Macduff's Invisible bagpipes." She fumbled around and picked them up. "He must have dropped them in the struggle," she said sadly, meeting Gus's eyes.

"I don't like it here in these gardens now they've all gone. It's horrible, waiting for them to catch us too."

They sat still and listened. Outside the Tower they could hear the murmurings of the leaves and trees as they worried amongst themselves. The whole Garden seemed to be waiting.

It was Gus who had a most uncomfortable thought. "What if they come back for us? What if they're waiting outside?"

Almost in answer they heard the distant chant of trees on the march

"Left Root
 Right Root
 Quick March Trees.
 Left Root
 Right Root
 Quick March Trees. Left Root...."

 "It's Them," squeaked Charlie, "It's the Pines. They're coming for us."

"You cannot really win can you? You have lost to Thoth."

Gus ran to the battlements and peered over. Far down below he could see a long line of Pine trees snaking towards the tower. There was no chance of escape. They were trapped.

A harsh voice shouted up. "Humans — You are surrounded. Surrender to Thoth. He will have mercy."

The trees behind him tittered softly and one or two began to shake with giggles.

"Mercy", scoffed Charlie, "Thoth?"

Gus stared at her and turned pale. "Remember that bit about Blood?"

Charlie climbed onto the stone seat and leaned over the wall.

"What have you done with our friends?"

A ripple of laughter passed through the leaves.

"Surrender," they shouted, "surrender. Thoth will have mercy."

"Silence," shouted the tallest tree and he turned his one eye upwards to where Charlie was watching. "Friends," he shouted, "A stone frog, a ridiculous bush, an invisible Scotsman? These are no friends for humans. Our Great, Gruesome Majesty, Lord Thoth of the Garden offers you His Awesome friendship. He wishes to meet you."

"And what if we don't choose to come down?" shouted Gus, "What if we say we will stay up here?"

"Come," shouted the tallest tree, "let us not be foolish. We are all reasonable beings. Join us and be with us. Otherwise,..."

"Tell them, Captain Needle, tell them."

"Silence," roared the tall tree.

"Otherwise," he continued, "we will be forced to climb the stairs and get you ourselves." The one dark eye swivelled upwards. "But you will join us, won't you?"

They looked at each other. "We may as well."

With sinking hearts and frightened faces they wound their way back down the stairs and walked outside into the fresh air to face a dark green Pine tree as tall as a house and covered with sharp needles that stuck out in all directions like a porcupine's quills.

The thin gash of a mouth opened and the tree spoke. "You cannot really win, can you? You have lost to Thoth." He turned around and winked at the other trees with his solitary eye. "And it may not be friendship that He offers you, after all. It may be.... something else."

Gus stepped forwards. "What have you done with our friends?"

A scarred, gnarled old Pine tree stepped forwards. "Tell them, Captain Needle," he growled, "tell them."

Captain Needle turned around and the thin gash curved slightly upwards in a cruel grin." We will let our Great Gruesome Majesty, Lord Thoth of the Garden tell them Himself. He will enjoy that."

The old, scarred tree moved smartly backwards into line.

Gus turned around. "I'm getting out of here."

"Arrest them," barked one of the trees and they both found themselves held in a tight grip.

"Ouch," said Charlie as a needle dug into her arm, "that hurt."

The black Pine pulled her tighter. "It was meant to," he sneered.

Charlie lashed out with her foot and stamped on one of the white, slug-like feet. "Take that," she gasped. But the Black Pine merely tightened his grip on her arm until tears started to her eyes.

Gus spoke, "don't struggle, Charlie — it only makes things worse. We'll have to go along with them. Look how many of them there are. We don't have a chance."

Captain Needle's black eye gleamed. "At least you show some sense," he said. "And now let us go to Thoth. We have wasted enough time. He will be getting impatient. Lead on."

Flat roots slapped smartly along the path, dragging the two children with them. They looked hopelessly at each other, dreading the Meeting.

CHAPTER 5

The Thing in the Cave

The trees dragged them along the path until they came to a flight of steep stone steps. Roughly they pushed Gus and Charlie up to the top, scratching them with their branches.

Either side of a stone path lay four stone sphinxes — statues with the bodies of lions but the faces of men. As the two children stumbled along, pushed by the trees, the nearest sphinx opened a cold grey eye.

"Who dares approach the Tomb of Thoth?"

"We have prisoners," crowed the trees.

"What kind of prisoners?" yawned the sphinx.

"Trespassers," chanted the Pines, "human children who entered the Gardens without our Great Gruesome Majesty's invite."

The scarred old Pine stepped forwards. "We have captured them to bring them to Thoth." And he pushed Gus and Charlie forwards so the Sphinx could rest his cold grey eye on them.

The Sphinx studied Gus for a long time and then wearily closed his eye. After a while he opened it again and this time stared at Charlie. Then he turned to the Pines. "Leave them," he said pompously. "I will take them to Thoth myself."

21

"Who dares approach the Tomb of Thoth?"

The Pines murmured amongst themselves. They had hoped to take all the credit for the capture but the Sphinx firmly fixed them with his cold stone eye. The Pines loosened their grip and bowed so low their tops swept the ground. Then they moved back in a long swaying line and swished away down the path leaving long dragging footprints in the turf.

The sphinx yawned and stood erect, his tail quivering high over the sleek body as daintily he stepped down from his pedestal.

"Follow me".

They looked desperately at one another but the sphinx turned and fixed his stoney stare at them. "I said, Follow Me." He led them towards a yawning black hole over which was a strange sign — two outstretched wings covered with weird picture writing. As they passed underneath them they felt queer — sick and dizzy. The sphinx turned and spoke. "You'll probably be feeling the effects of the Black Magic about now," he said casually, "it'll pass off soon. Oh — and by the way." He waved one razor sharp claw in front of their eyes, "You won't forget to bow, will you. His Great Gruesome Majesty absolutely loathes folks who haven't got the manners to bow when they meet a Superior Being." They shook their heads, still feeling dizzy and sick and followed the haughty shape of the sphinx into the black nothing.

They couldn't see a thing but stumbled slowly along the passage, their hands outstretched ahead of them. Gus felt something cold and slimey against his hand and withdrew it sharply. As they moved along behind the padding footsteps of the Spinx they felt a blast of ice-cold air rush past their ears — and with it was a foul stench of rotting vegetables. Still they moved forwards.

A voice thundered along the passage. "Who dares enter the Tomb of Thoth?"

"It's only me," said the Sphinx in his quiet voice. "I have here the two human children, your Great Gruesome Majesty. The Pines arrested them in the Watch Tower and brought them to me."

"Good," thundered the voice. "Bring them forwards, Sekmet."

"Look," whispered Gus and he grabbed hold of Charlie's arm, "Look." In the blackness ahead two red eyes glowed like hot coals. Gus swallowed.

In the red glow they could see a fat, squat shape. As their eyes became accustomed to the dark they made out more — a white flash of sharp teeth and they saw Thoth standing in front of them.

HE WAS AN APE.

He was short, fat, black and hairy. His eyes were red and his nose squashed quite flat to his face. Between two thick, ugly lips they caught a flash of sharp white teeth. He smelt horrible, dead fish, stale cabbage and overfull dustbins.

AND HE WAS UGLY.

Thoth leaned forwards so that his hairy belly flopped on his knees. "Bow," ordered the Sphinx and he pushed them in the small of their backs so they fell on their faces to the floor of the cave. Charlie spat out a mouthful of damp soil. "Ugh."

"That's better," purred the Sphinx and Thoth gave a snort of approval.

23

He was an Ape.

"You are spies," growled Thoth.

"Oh no..."

"Your Great Gruesome Majesty," prompted the Sphinx. "Give Thoth his proper title."

"Your Great Gruesome Majesty... We are not spies," stammered out Gus.

"You sought, with your friends, to overthrow ME." said Thoth. Gus fell quiet.

"You plotted against me with that wretched Frog."

"No...No.... At least... not really."

"What brought you to my domain?" asked Thoth, moving forwards on fat squat legs with knees like two black footballs.

"We simply climbed over the wall." Charlie had found her voice. Thoth studied fat black fingers. "How many of you are there?"

"Only two."

The two red eyes glowed in the gloom and Thoth stared. "And who exactly knows you are here?"

Gus was suddenly wary. "Loads of people."

"Who?"

"Our parents. They'll send out a search party if we don't get back soon." Gus was really wishing he had told his parents where he was.

24

"I am ruler here," snarled Thoth. "I own these Gardens. All within the Great Walls of China are mine. You are here. Therefore you too are mine. Do you understand, humans?"

He reached out one repulsive hand and stroked Charlie's cheek. She shrank.

"Why don't you join me, little girl?"

She shook her head dumbly. The repulsive hand pinched her hard so she almost screamed. "Never," she managed to stammer.

"Never?" He roared, "**never**... Never is an awfully long time. How would you like to be locked up in this place and I say you will **never** be released? Or that you will **never** again see your parents? **Never** is not a word to be spoken lightly. I think..." A fat hand stroked his triple chin, "... I think I will keep you here until you decide to.... co-operate." He turned aside to Sekmet, and spoke in a low voice. "Fetch me a knife, will you, and make it a good sharp one." His eyes rested on the two children and glowed blood-red. "Why don't you sit down," he said with a leer, "and make yourselves comfortable."

Gus turned to Charlie. "We've got to get out of here — quickly."

She stared. "How?"

It was then that he saw it — a narrow sliver of light shining underneath what just might be a door. He stared at it. Was it a door? He peered closer and made out what just might be a key. Then again — it might not.

Up the corridor they heard Sekmet's quiet footsteps padding back. It was now or never. He prodded Charlie. "Over there," he whispered, "I think it's a door."

Her eyes followed the direction and she nodded.

He stood up. "Now," he shouted and they both ran. Gus found the key first and struggled to turn it. Behind them they heard the Beast roar and Sekmet snarl. The key turned. They flung the door open and ran out to daylight.

"Shut it," Charlie hissed and they pulled it tightly behind them, turning the key and locking it. Only then did they dare to breathe again.

Charlie looked around her. "Now where?"

"Here." Gus pointed to a steep narrow flight of steps with a door at the top. "Come on."

They belted up the steps, expecting the door at the top to be locked. It wasn't. It was open. They pushed it open further and ran through.

CHAPTER 6
The Universal Grandmother

They found themselves in a small room with a high, beamed ceiling. It was quite empty apart from a long wooden table up the centre and a bench. At the far end of the room, underneath an arched window, stood an old woman bending over a stove with a long wooden spoon in her hand. As they ran in she turned and smiled.

"Hello, my dears," she said, "I was wonderin' when you'd pop by and pay me a visit."

They were too surprised and out of breath to say a word.

She turned back to the stove and stirred something in a blackened old saucepan. "Nasty piece of work, isn't he?"

Still they said nothing. The old woman wiped her hands down a spotless white apron that almost swept the floor and smiled, her face cracking into a thousand wrinkles.

Charlie was the first to recover her voice. "Who are you?" The old woman didn't answer for a moment. She was fetching out two tin dishes from the bottom of the stove.

"Well," she pondered, "think of me as a sort of Universal Grandmother — the sort that children can come to when they've got a bit of a problem." Her eyes twinkled. "And if I'm not very much mistaken, you two young chickens have got a bit of a problem, haven't you?"

"Why does her voice remind me of treacle?" whispered Gus.

"Oh," carried on the Grandmother comfortably, it's rich and sweet the same as the way I talk. Why don't you two come and sit down and have a bowl of broth?"

"What about Thoth?" Gus asked, nervously glancing at the door.

"Don't you worry your heads about that old monkey," said the Universal Grandmother putting two steaming bowls of stew down in front of them, "his powers don't work in 'ere." She chuckled. "If they did I'd have bin a gonner long ago."

She sat down beside them on the bench and watched them taste the stew. "Tasty enough for you?"

"Oh yes."

"You see, as long as I stay in 'ere in the Cheshire Cottage I'm safe. However..." She broke off as a large pink tongue appeared a little above her right shoulder. "There you are, Cheese," she said severely, "I haven't seen you all afternoon. Where have you been?"

Around the pink tongue grew a wide grinning mouth and eight quivering whiskers.

"Cheese", said the old woman slowly turning pink with embarrassment "it isn't good manners to only half appear before guests. Show yourself immediately."

She looked apologetically at Gus and Charlie. "I'm sorry," she said, "this cat of mine has no manners at all."

Below the whiskers grew a fat tabby face then a furry neck and two front paws. Next came a plump body and last of all a long twitching tail that appeared, quite strangely at the twitch and grew until it met the body. It was a fascinating sight. The cat floated gently downwards and padded softly towards a saucer of milk in the corner.

"She reminds me of the Sphinx," Charlie commented.

The cat turned around. It's yellow eyes gleamed and her tail twitched. She said nothing but quietly lapped at the saucer of milk with her long tongue.

Charlie looked intently around her at the room with its low beamed ceiling, the blackened stove, the broom that leaned against the corner and finally at the old woman with her wrinkled face like a hankie that no-one had ironed. "It's awfully funny," she said slowly, "but I have the weirdest feeling that I've been here before."

"I feel like that," said Gus, "but we haven't, have we?"

The Universal Grandmother didn't seem in the least bit surprised.

"Pickle Jars," she said.

"I beg your pardon," Gus said politely, "did you say pickle jars?"

"Yes," said the Grandmother comfortably, "that's what I said. Pickle Jars. Your minds, you two, are like store cupboards. Things are there, right at the back sometimes but there all the same. You may have been here, perhaps in a dream. And you've forgotten, but it's stayed, tucked away behind all the things you need to know for every day, like how many tens are in a hundred or what day your mother's birthday is. But right at the back, neatly stored in a pickle jar is an old dream of such a place as you might visit one day. Pickle Jars."

"But Pickle jars or no pickle jars you can only store things that have actually happened," objected Gus.

"I've never thought that," said the Universal Grandmother. "Pickle jars are full of all sorts of things that might happen. Understand?"

"Pickle jars."

And they all laughed suddenly, as though pickle jars were the funniest things in the world.

"Did you know we were coming?"

The Universal Grandmother gave a knowing wink. "I rather think I did," she said, "it was in one of my pickle jars."

27

The cat miawoed suddenly and leaped up onto the Universal Grandmother's lap. She stroked her fur. "My little Cheese," she said.

"My little Cheese," she said.

28

"Why do you call her Cheese?" Charlie was curious; it seemed a strange name for a cat.

"Well she's a Cheshire cat," she said, "Cheshire cat, Cheshire Cheese." And they all laughed again.

"And now," said the old lady, "it's time to talk."

Cheese's ears pricked up and she stopped purring. The Universal Grandmother carried on stroking her.

"You were running away, weren't you?"

They nodded.

"And you want to know where your friends are, don't you?"

The cat's ears twitched sharply.

"I'm afraid I don't know," she said, "but I can put you in touch with someone who will. Do you know the Cave?"

"Yes." Gus remembered. "We hid there one time when we were hiding from the Pines."

"Four bats live there. They will know what has happened to your friends. But make quite sure no-one sees you. This Garden is full of enemies and spies. You can trust no-one." She stroked the cat gently and Cheese narrowed her eyes and pretended to purr. "You'd better go straight away. Move quickly and quietly. If you hear the Pines take cover. They'll be all over the Gardens looking for you."

"When you do find your friends," she continued, "go at once to the Willow Pattern Garden and consult the Wise Mandarin who lives in the Joss House. If the Red Ox challenges you or the Gateway Dragons start breathing their smokey fire all over you, just tell them the Universal Grandmother sent you and use my password."

"What's that?"

"Pickle jars of course," chuckled the old woman. "They won't hurt you if you just say 'Pickle jars'. They'll know who sent you. I think the Mandarin will be able to help you overthrow Thoth. He's very old, I know, but he used to have a special book all about the Gardens. The Book of Owls it's called. Consult that and I think you'll have an answer. Now, you'd better hurry or the Pines will guess you're here and surround the cottage. Cheese will take you to the Bat's Cave." She looked around her. "Cheese," she called. "Cheese. Where are you?"

"Where is that cat?" she said crossly. "I do wish she wouldn't keep disappearing all the time."

The door swung gently open and closed again. No-one noticed it.

The Universal Grandmother shook her head. "I just do not know where that cat gets to all the time. She just ups and offs." She turned back to the children. "Well you two haven't got time to hang around. You must find your way on your own. I can't show you. I can't leave the cottage."

She smiled. "Good luck," she said. "And remember — Pickle Jars."

29

CHAPTER 7

The Cave of Bats

They crept out of the cottage, listening for the sound of those flat roots slapping over the path. Twice Charlie grabbed Gus's arm, thinking she saw a bush move. "Something's watching us, Gus, I'm sure."

Something was watching them.

"Let's hurry." Gus held his sister's arm and they hurried along the path, towards the oak tree with a split trunk.

A sudden swish of tree roots made them dive for cover behind a moss covered rock. They peered around to see four Pines swaying along the path. As they passed, one of the trees spoke and they recognized the old, scarred Pine that had been with Captain Needle earlier. "We must find them or Thoth will be angry. He will chop us up and feed us to the Fires."

"We will find them," said another. "If they are still in the Garden we will get them in the end."

"In the end," echoed another.

Gus and Charlie cowered lower behind the rock until the trees were out of sight. Then they ran through the stone arch and finally reached the Cave of Bats.

. . . .

With her tail held high, Cheese was approaching the avenue of Sphinxes.

"Who goes there?" Sekmet had noticed her.

"It is I," purred the cat, twitching her tail confidently. "It is I, sacred and favoured cat, Pet of Thoth the Ruler. Let me pass, stone cousin."

The Sphinx blinked.

"Come along," purred the cat, "you stone apology for a lion. Let me pass."

The Sphinx looked angry and inclined his head. "Pass then, Cheshire cat. But mind the blood of a human does not touch me or I shall surely be a true lion and then it will be the worse for you, my little pussy cat."

Sekmet stretched out one long, sharp claw. "For now, Cheese, you may enter." And the cat walked between the four sphinxes with a proud, haughty walk, tail twitching and her sly, yellow eyes narrowed to slits.

She padded straight up the black corridor towards the red glow at the end. When she reached it she folded her two front paws in front of her and bent her head to the floor.

"I have news, Great Gruesome Master," she purred.

The Ape clenched his fist. "What news, Favoured One?"

"The human children," miaowed the cat, "they plan to set the others free — the frog, Bracken, the bush, Bilberry and the Scotsman, Macduff."

The Ape scratched his head. "How?"

"I don't know yet," said the cat, "but the Universal Grandmother has told them to go to the Cave of Bats and they are on their way there now."

"That interfering old bag?" roared the ape.

The cat flashed her claws out. "Why not let me deal with her, master?" and she dragged her claws along the floor of the tunnel with a harsh rasping noise.

The ape bent his fat neck towards the cat. "You would enjoy that, wouldn't you?"

The cat grinned. "Oh...yes. The Universal Old Bag thinks to rule ME when I have only one real Master, Oh Great One."

"At least you are loyal," murmured the ape, stroking his triple chin.

The cat said nothing.

"Then," roared the ape, throwing back his head and shouting with laughter," do with her as you wish, Cheese." And he and the cat made the cave ring with the echoes of their laughter.

"But first," said the Ape when they had both stopped laughing, "make yourself invisible and follow the children. I sense a threat there, listen to all their conversation and report anything important straight back to me."

The cat purred contentedly, and slowly in the red glow she began to disappear — tail first. It twitched and was gone. Then the fat furry body starting at the bottom and finishing at the sleek neck.

"Farewell, Master," said the mouth. Then that was gone too. And all that was heard was a quick swish as Cheese left the Tunnel.

The Ape sat still for a while, nothing moving except the short black hairs on the back of his neck which twitched, then he jerked into action. "Captain Needle, I have need of you. Arm your men."

· · · · · · · · · ·

Meanwhile Gus and Charlie had reached the entrance to the bat's cave, panting and breathless from running more than half the way. The cave looked blacker than they remembered — and darker too.

31

Now that the moment had come they felt uneasy. What if the bats weren't in? Gus stepped into the entrance.

"Hello", he called, "is anyone there?"

There was a flutter of leathery wings and a voice squeaked angrily. "Can't a chap have any sleep these days?"

"The Universal Grandmother sent us," Charlie called into the echoing cave. "She said you would help us find Bracken and the others."

"Well don't just stand there," squeaked the voice, "come inside. It's safer."

Gus struck a match and lit a candle and the inside of the cave glowed. Four bats were hanging upside down from the roof, watching them curiously with tiny black eyes.

"My name's Clap," said the largest dropping down beside them on the floor.

"My name is Trap," said the smallest.

"I'm Rag..."

"And I'm Bag," said the other two and they grinned at them the way that bats do.

"Do you know where Bracken and the others are?"

The four bats all started squeaking in high pitched voices in a strange tongue then Clap spoke again. "We think we can trust you," he said. "In these troubled times it can be very hard to know who your real friends are, but we have decided to take you into our confidence." He looked sad. "So many have joined Thoth."

"They were rounded up," said Rag a brown bat with tangled fur, "marooned on the island in the centre of the lily lake. Weeping Holly told us an hour ago. Captain Needle took them there on a boat and then brought the boat back so they could not get off. They intend leaving them there without food until they surrender."

"Could we get them off?" asked Gus.

"Can you handle a boat?"

"Sssh," whispered Trap the smallest bat, a small hairy thing with soft brown fur and huge ears. "Did you hear that — what was it?"

They all listened. Outside there was a soft soft shuffle. It was so quiet you could barely call it a sound; it was more a movement of air. But they heard it all the same. And it frightened them. Even more because it was so stealthy. Then they heard another sound which they recognized. It was the rattle of Pine Needles.

"It's them," whispered Clap, looking hard at them. "How did they know where to find you?"

"Were you followed?" asked Rag

They shook their heads. "We were awfully careful. I'm sure no one saw us enter the cave but the question is," said Charlie "how do we leave the cave."

32

"Create a diversion."

"Strategy," squeaked Trap the smallest bat excitedly, "What we need is strategy."

"Right," said Clap, the big brown bat, "I will fly to the entrance and see how many there are of the blighters. Then.." his eyes gleamed, "...we can plan."

He flew silently along the roof of the cave towards the mouth and was back in a trice. "Three."

"Now," he said, taking charge. "You, Trap, must lead the children to the boat. It's tied underneath the *Weeping Holly" he added. "Take the boat to the island and get Bracken, Bilberry and Macduff off. The rest of us must distract the Pines so Gus and Charlie can slip away unnoticed. Understand?"

They all nodded.

"Right," he said, "we will go out first. When you hear the trees start to shriek, slip away. We'll draw them far away from the entrance. Take your chance, you two, don't miss us. And..." He looked at them kindly, "..good luck."

He puffed out his furry chest and raised one black leathery wing in command. "Right, Bats, Ready... Steady... To your stations and Go - o - O."

Three of the bats flew along the roof of the cave, sharp teeth bared. They were ready to do battle.

In a moment those inside the cave heard sounds — "Ouch" and "What's that?" and one or two "Helps."

Trap looked at the children and grinned. "Come on, time to leave."

They sneaked out of the Cave of Bats, blinking at the bright sunshine after the gloom of the cave. A little along the path they could see the three Pines with the bats fluttering around them, beating them with their wings. Gus and Charlie watched for no more than a second then ran in the opposite direction, Trap leading the way, hearing the shrieks of Clap urging the bats to attack. "Beat them, lads, show them no mercy. Bite them."

They ran along the path until they could just see the pale glisten of water through the trees. Charlie stopped for a moment. "What's that?"

They all stopped and listened. Something — or someone, was sobbing loudly right in front of them.

"That's her," said Trap, "That's Weeping Holly."

*N.B. No, I do not mean a Weeping Willow. One hundred and twenty years ago Mr. Bateman planted a Weeping Holly in The Garden.

CHAPTER 8

Rescue

The sobs grew louder and louder as they approached the lake with the overgrown island in the centre. But they couldn't see so much as a sign of their three friends.

Trap led them to a wide Holly tree whose branches dangled right to the ground. Charlie touched one of the glistening leaves. "It's wet," she said.

"Tears," explained Trap. "Weeping Holly spends most of her time crying about something or other." He parted the dangling branches and they followed him inside.

"Hello there, Weeping Holly."

"Hello Trap," the tree sobbed and a few more tears fell to the ground which was already soaking wet. "Oh poor Bracken, poor Bilberry, poor Macduff — they're stranded now. No one will ever get them off that island. If they try they'll sink into the Beneath World and no-one ever gets out of there alive. It's impossible for them to swim. If they try they'll drown and who can manage a boat? They'll starve to death." She shook her branches.

"Look out," said Trap getting a little impatient, "you're practically drowning me."

"They were my best friends," wailed the tree.

"Look here," said Trap, "I've brought two children. They're our friends. They can manage a boat. They'll have them all off the island in no time. No time at all."

"They'll never manage it," sobbed the tree. "It's too far and Bracken will sink the boat. He's too heavy. He'll sink you all into the Beneath World."

Gus glanced at Charlie anxiously. The 'Beneath World' sounded very uninviting.

"Don't be so pessimistic," said Trap sharply. "They're going to try which is more than you've done, wrapping your roots around you and howling all day. What good is that going to do? Such a noise," he scolded, "and all for nothing. Really, Holly," he said severely, "I'm quite ashamed of you. Now let us have a council of war and work something out."

Weeping Holly gave a loud sniff and shook her branches. "Sit down," she said, "be my guests."

They sat down on a rock and she pulled her long, dangling branches together so they were quite enclosed and hidden from view. They were in a dark green private room. They could not see out and they could not be seen — but they could be heard. And they were.

Weeping Holly's mournful brown eyes rested on Gus and Charlie. "I'm sorry," she said, "but I'm always miserable, aren't I, Trap?"

Trap rolled his eyes impatiently.

"You see life has been hard for me. Many things have happened and all of them tragic......"

"No time for all that," said Trap leaping to his feet. "We want action. Where is the boat for us to cross to the island?"

Holly began to wail again. "But they might sink it, and drown."

Charlie smiled. "It's all right, Holl," she said. "We can both swim really well and it's the only way to rescue our friends."

"Sure?" sobbed Holly. "The lake is bottomless you know."

"Yes," said Gus, trying hard not to think of the Beneath World.

Holly wriggled her trunk and a piece of rope that was tied around her middle loosened and came free. "Grab that," she said. "It's tied to the boat."

They pulled the rope and followed it down to the water's edge where a small, neat blue boat was sitting bobbing up and down on the water.

"Great." Trap rubbed his leathery wings together and looked pleased. "Ship Ahoy. Now climb in and we'll get going. Any moment now the Pines will be after us."

Holly wailed after them. "Please ... be careful. You'll sink if you don't watch it."

"Shut up." Trap had had enough.

They rowed quickly towards the centre of the lake, Gus peering down through the water. It seemed to make a strange sound, a sort of loud wailing and moaning.

"The Beneath World," said Trap. "Let's hurry up."

"What are those?" Charlie pointed up to some tiny fairies dressed in pinks and white, chattering and giggling as they surrounded the boat.

Trap looked furious. "It's those wretched Lily Fairies," he said crossly, "Trust them to come and make a nuisance of themselves."

"But they're so pretty," said Charlie, "and what's that song they're singing? Listen."

Across the water came the sound of silvery sweet voices singing as the Lily Fairies sang and twirled their skirts. The children listened to the song.

"We laugh — we sing — we play on air
We Lily Fairies have no care
We're never sad 'cos that's not our way
We never work — we only play
Life's for living — life's for fun
So come and join us everyone."

"We laugh — we sing — we play on air. We Lily Fairies have no care!"

"No use," grumbled Trap, "they're no use at all." He climbed to the prow of the boat. "Will you please be quiet," he shouted, "I can't steer straight with all the din you're making."

36

The Lily Fairies took absolutely no notice but simply collapsed into fresh gales of laughter and they waved and pointed their toes and carried on twirling around the boat until Gus felt quite dizzy.

"Not much good at rowing, are you?" They giggled and nudged each other, holding their skirts daintily above the water.

Now even Gus was annoyed. "Be quiet, will you?"

They tried to ignore the Lily Fairies and rowed the boat nearer and nearer the island with the cloud of Lily Fairies fluttering around them, giggling each time they got stuck or tangled with the oars.

"Go and find somebody else to plague," Trap yelled angrily, "Leave us alone." But the Lily Fairies took no notice.

It was as they drew nearer the island and could make out a small cove where they could land that they at last caught sight of Bracken, sitting dejectedly on a stone with Bilberry flopped on a nearby patch of grass. They shouted delightedly.

"Bracken, Bilberry..."

Bracken's yellow eyes blinked happily at them. "Gus, Charlie," and he hopped along the bank in long jerky steps shouting at them all the time.

"Bilberry, Macduff, look who's here. It's the children. I told you they wouldn't abandon us."

Bilberry scuttled out, her twigs flying all over the place and her green socks bright against the grey stone. "Hello," she called, jumping up and down. And from behind came the deep booming voice of Macduff. "I'm powerful glad to see you two. I was just beginnin' to get really hungry. And what's more, I've lost ma bagpipes."

"We found them" Charlie said happily as they docked the boat. "They were on the floor in the Watch Tower. We put them in the corner. They should be perfectly safe."

"Guid," said Macduff, "you are a Bonny and True Lassie." Charlie blushed.

Bracken grinned his wide, ugly smile. "If I was still a real frog I would have been off this island in no time at all. But..." And he sat down on the stone and looked sad.

Bilberry sat next to him. "I never learnt to swim." She scratched the top of her head. "Come to that," she added thoughtfully, "I don't think many bushes can."

"Well," piped up Macduff from somewhere near, "I could quite easily have swum to safety — even though I would have gotten ma kilt a wee bit wet. But leave ma friends? ...NEVER." And he thumped his foot down and left a huge footprint in the soil.

"We ought to hurry up and leave," Gus said seriously. "They might come back and start looking for us. Besides", he added, "we have a message for you from the Universal Grandmother."

Bracken blinked. "You met her?" he asked. "But she never leaves the cottage — at least not since I can remember."

"We've got an awful lot to tell you," Charlie said. "But it had better wait until we're back on the mainland."

They all climbed back in the boat which sank frighteningly low in the water and Gus was afraid might sink with the extra weight of the stone frog in. Trap flew on ahead and spyed out for any Pines or other enemies. Gus took one of the oars and Macduff held the other. (It looked very odd, swishing through the water with no-one holding it.) They hadn't gone out very far before the Lily Fairies once again clustered around them and began to laugh.

Bracken looked at them severely. "I'm ashamed of you," he scolded, "laughing at folks in trouble. Why don't you help?"

One of the Lily Fairies in a dress of sparkling silver tissue hovered over his head. "Because we don't know what else to do. We meant no harm Bracken. But we too are afraid of Thoth. We have no power; we are not clever." Her lovely face grew sad.

"But there is something you can do," said the frog. "You can skim over the water and watch for the Pines. You can warn Holly that we are coming back. You can guide us into the channel where we can land safest."

The silver fairy listened attentively and then in one soft cloud the Lily Fairies flew off and were gone. In a few moments they were all back. "We see no-one," she said, "and the Holly awaits your return."

"There" said Bracken, grinning widely, "there is always something you can do. It's just that you have to try hard to find it, sometimes."

"Bracken," Gus said urgently, "the boat's in trouble."

At the bottom of the boat where they had not noticed it before, two of the planks were a little loose. Through the hole seeped water. And the boat was already low. They were sinking. And as they floated lower in the water, the Beneath World seemed to know and suck them down.

Bracken looked desperately at the boy. "It's my weight," he said sadly. "It's causing you to sink."

Gus nodded. "But not far to go."

"We won't make it," said Bracken, sadly. "There's only one thing to do to make sure you all get to the other side safely." He stood up and before anyone could say another word, dived over the side. They all stared, too shocked to say a word. The dark oily waters of the Beneath World closed over him and there was a shout of glee from deep down below.

They stared at each other horrified. "Bracken," Charlie whispered.

38

Bilberry screamed. "Bracken, my friend. Bracken, oh Bracken." and she put her head on Charlie's shoulder and howled.

The little boat bobbed to the side and they all sat, motionless, too miserable to move.

"Come along," said Macduff at last, "we have work to do."

They tied the rope around Holly's side and told her quietly what had happened. For a while her branches waved around hopelessly then teardrops appeared on her leaves and silently dripped to the floor. "Poor Bracken. And now how will you defeat Thoth? Give yourselves up? Throw yourselves on his mercy? He will soon come with his army of trees — and his cruelty ...." Her voice faded away. "Whose side are you on?" Macduff's gruff voice chimed in. "Wretched tree can you never be more cheerful?"

Holly gave a loud groan.

They were all so busy listening to Holly and Macduff that none of them saw the trailing branches part for a moment and two sly yellow eyes peer around the fronds. No-one noticed the spiteful grin — or the twitching tail. And before anyone saw her, Cheese melted away into the distance.

CHAPTER 9

The Plan

For a while they were all too upset at Bracken's disappearance into the Beneath World to do anything else but sit around, staring at one another then Macduff's gruff voice spoke up.

"Did you say you'd met the Universal Grandmother? I haven't seen her in years. How is she these dark days?"

"She's all right," Charlie said, "she gave us a bowl of broth?"

"Aye, she's a guid cook. How did you come to meet her?"

"We were taken by the trees," began Gus.

"The Sphinx, Sekmet, took us to Thoth."

"You saw him?" Bilberry's face paled.

Gus and Charlie nodded. "Yes."

"We ran through a door..."

"and up some steps..."

"Somehow we found ourselves in a cottage and she was there, cooking."

"Now that's typical for you to find her when you need her most. That's the sort of person she is."

"She told us to go to the Willow Pattern Garden and speak to the Mandarin who lives in the Joss House."

"The Red Ox won't let you through," squeaked Bilberry.

"She gave us a password."

"Pickle jars," finished Charlie.

"I dunna like goin' past those dragons. They stop you gettin' anywhere near the Joss House."

"She said the password would work on them too."

"Trap fluttered through the trailing branches. "I'd better be getting back to the Cave of Bats," he said. "They might be having trouble."

"Of course." Gus turned to the bat. "Thanks ever so much, Trap. We couldn't have managed without you."

The bat flew out of the tree room — and almost brushed a twitching whisker. But he didn't notice a thing.

"Right then," Gus stood up. "Time to consult the mandarin. Lead on Macduff." (He had grown quite used to the invisible piper by now and almost never forgot that he was there — by various signs, cushions of flattened turf, the parting of branches and leaves, by the long footprints that appeared wherever the ground was soft. Charlotte too found it quite ordinary now having a friend who could not be seen — except for one thing. She was unbearably curious to know what he looked like. She knew it was rude to ask but she couldn't help wondering.)

Charlie caught up with Macduff's footprints as they walked along the path. "Macduff," she asked, "who is the Mandarin? What does he look like and why do they call it the Willow Pattern Garden?"

"The Willow Pattern Garden was copied from a large Chinese plate, a little bridge over a lake and in the background a small joss house. Mr. Bateman, who built the Gardens, eventually traced a fine old Joss House in the Northern regions of China but it was lived in by a wise old hermit. However Mr. Bateman decided that he must have the Joss House, hermit or not. So he offered the old man a permanent home here on condition that he could bring the Joss House back to the Gardens. That was how they got here. You see, the mandarin didn't really care where his Joss House was. He never went outside anyway."

"How strange," said Gus.

Charlie skipped along the path quickly, anxious to reach the Joss House and the Mandarin to see if there was any way they might be able to enter the Beneath World and bring Bracken back to the Gardens. Then they could beat Thoth and get rid of his rotten presence. She wouldn't have been so hopeful if she could have seen inside the Tomb of Thoth.

. . . .

"Great Gruesome Majesty," purred Cheese, licking her lips in anticipation, "they have rescued the prisoners from the island."

"What?" roared the ape.

"But the frog left the boat and sank to the Beneath World."

The Ape chuckled and rubbed his hands together. "Good".

"Holly Tree was with them," snarled the cat.

"We will burn her," roared Thoth.

"It was the bat that guided them."

The Ape's eye gleamed in the darkness.

"Burn the tree," he muttered, "kill the bat. Roast it on her embers. Smoke the cave, seal the entrance, choke the other members." He laughed cruelly. "It will be fun to watch them cough and splutter in the smoke. The Pines may do it this very afternoon."

The cat grinned and ran her tongue over dry lips. "Cream?" she purred.

Thoth's eyes burned into hers. "You would do anything for cream wouldn't you, Cheese?"

"Cream?" the cat purred again.

"Firstly tell me where they are now."

The cat's tail twitched. "They go to consult the Mandarin."

"That old Chinese Ancient," thundered Thoth, "I thought he had kicked the bucket years ago."

"I believe," snarled the cat, "that he still lives."

The Ape stroked his three fat chins. "So what if they have?" he sneered, "what good can that fat old man and his crazy assistant do? Nothing — Nothing against MY Greatness. Let them go," he bellowed. "It will do ME no harm."

The cat edged towards the saucer of cream. "And the old woman?" Her eyes narrowed to two narrow strips of yellow.

"Stay your hand — we may have further need of you yet."

"Sekmet ... Sekmet," he called, "get a saucer of cream" and the cat licked her whiskers in anticipation.

. . . .

"To get to the Chinese garden we have to walk through the cave of Bats. It'll be dark. Slip your hand in mine, Wee Lassie."

"Macduff," Charlie said, "how do you think the Mandarin will be able to help us?"

"We-e-ell, more than anyone else he knows the legends of the Gardens. He is the only one to have read the Book of Owls from cover to cover. I don't rightly know how but I think he will know of some way to get rid of Thoth for once and for all. He's our only hope."

They came out of the cave into the blinding sunlight and found their way blocked by a huge tree. They stared up at it. This wasn't a Pine. It was a quite different sort of tree. He was very tall and straight and his branches were weird twisted shapes with short spikey points on them. His feet were two dark lumpy roots and on his head he wore a bowler hat. This he swept off and bowed deeply.

"Great," he said, rubbing his prickles together. "Now for some fun."

"Oh not today, Monkey Puzzle," squeaked Bilberry nervously, "We haven't got the time. We're in trouble and in a hurry. We've got to get through to the Mandarin."

Monkey Puzzle looked sulky. "I won't let you pass."

"No. We haven't got time." Gus stepped forward. "We're in a hurry."

"It won't take long."

"NO."

Monkey Puzzle gave them a mean look. "You can't pass unless you play."

"Play what?"

"Riddles"

CHAPTER 10
Monkey Puzzle

"Tell you what," said the Monkey Puzzle tree with a sneer, "as you're in a hurry, I'll let you have first go."

Gus scratched his head. "I'm not much good at riddles."

"Me neither," Macduff's voice chimed in.

"And I'm not much better," Bilberry squeaked. "What are you like at riddles, Charlie?"

"Luckily, not bad. Are you ready Monkey Puzzle?" (She loved puzzles, had done ever since she was three years old. And she knew a good one that was absolutely bound to fox the tree.)

"In comes two legs carrying one leg which he lays down on three legs. Out goes two legs. Up jumps four legs and runs off with one leg. Back comes two legs, snatches up three legs and throws it after four legs to get back one leg."

Monkey Puzzle leaned one way then another and scratched the top of his head with one spikey green branch. "That's a difficult one, little girl," he said sharply, "very difficult."

Charlie winked at the others and waited.

And waited.

And the tree thought.

And thought.

"Aha," he said at last, "I think I have it."

"Oh," they all said, disappointed.

"Is this it? — A man walks in with a leg of lamb." His eyes gleamed. "Am I on the right track?"

"Yes," said Charlie.

"He lays it down on a stool." Monkey Puzzle grinned, "a three legged stool. He goes out." He scratched his head. "Now where was I? Ah yes — Four legs picks up one leg. A dog runs in picks up the lamb and runs away with it. The man returns, picks up the three-legged stool and throws it at the dog to make him drop the lamb. How's that?"

"Very good," said Charlie, wishing he would move out of the way so they would get to the mandarin in the Joss House.

"Now I'll tell you one," said Monkey Puzzle, "and if you get it right you can go through."

He thought for a moment then gave a sly grin. He could beat her with this one. (He didn't know Charlie.)

"A-hem." He cleared his throat and spoke in a fast squeaky voice "I am but small, but when entire,

Of force to set a town on fire.

Let but one letter disappear
I then can hold a herd of deer.
Take one more off and then you'll find
I once contained all Mankind."

They all looked at one another. It sounded impossible. They groaned. Monkey Puzzle Tree giggled.

Then Charlie had a brainwave. She knew the answer.

(Have a guess yourselves and read down the page when you think you know the answer too.)

"Spark," she shouted. "When but small, but entire sets a town on fire."

"Park" can hold a herd of deer.

"Ark" held all Mankind.

"I say," said Monkey Puzzle admiringly, "very good... very good indeed." He moved sideways. "You can pass," he said, "you've earned it."

"Thanks — and here's one to be thinking of while I'm gone," called back Charlie. "Little Miss Netticoat in a white petticoat and a red nose. She has no feet or hands and the longer she stands the shorter she grows.*"

Monkey Puzzle stood and scratched his head and the party of friends moved on leaving him still puzzling.

*A lit candle

CHAPTER 11

Orbis

"Isn't it beautiful," breathed Charlie.

They were standing in front of a small blue painted pagoda, overlooking the prettiest Willow Pattern Garden. Dainty fronds dipped down to a calm blue pool over which arched a small wooden bridge. Just at the top of a small flight of steps stood their object — the joss house.

"We have to go this way first," said Bilberry, "through the arch and past the two dragons and Orbis."

Immediately they passed through the stone arch draped with long whiskers of moss, two dragons sprang up and hissed long licks of blue flame towards them. "Halt," they said. "We are here to guard the Willow Pattern Garden. Who are you? Strangers, explain yourselves."

Gus stepped forward bravely. "The Universal Grandmother sent us," he said, "armed only with the password — Pickle Jars. We come to consult the Mandarin. Let us pass."

"I," said the ox pompously, "am Orbis."

"Sorry," said the dragons, hastily drawing in their tongues, "We were sure it was an enemy. You see, we heard the Pines were on the move."

"They are." A voice spoke from the top of the wall and to everyone's amazement a large red ox put her front hooves on the wall behind the dragons. "Who on earth are these?" She said haughtily, staring at the children with huge brown eyes.

"Who are you?" asked Charlie.

"I," said the ox pompously, "am Orbis. Between my horns I hold the sun, between my hooves lies the earth."

"I don't see any sun between your horns," Gus said curiously.

"Somebody stole it," said the ox, "and if I catch the blighter I'll... I'll..." She stopped for a minute.

"I watch over the Willow Pattern Gardens," she continued, "and decide who can see the Mandarin."

"We must see him," said Gus.

"What about?"

"We have to do something about that awful Thoth." They all turned around sharply. It was all too easy to forget about Macduff sometimes.

"Do something? What?"

"That's what we need to see the Mandarin about." Charlie was getting impatient with all the delays.

"You may pass," the red ox said after a little pause. "The Mandarin will help you."

A spiteful grin hovered in the air a little behind Macduff. "So," mused Cheese, "they have got here after all." A mean smile hovered on her face, "all except that idiot frog. Hmm... Much good that old twit of a Chinaman will do them, I'm sure. He must be at least a hundred. I think I'll just pop back to the Tomb and see what Thoth has to say about all this." Her tail swished through the air and her grin gradually faded. And still no one saw her.

CHAPTER 12
The Mandarin and the Book of Owls

They left Orbis and the two dragons and slowly climbed the steps to the wooden Joss House. When they reached the door, all four of them felt suddenly shy. "You knock," squeaked Bilberry. Gus glanced at the brass knocker.

"O.K."

He lifted it and dropped it twice and then they all stood back to wait.

From deep inside they heard the sound of rusty hinges being pulled squeakily back then the slow creak of a door being opened — a door that hadn't been opened for a very long time. Four and a half years actually.

A man stood there.

I say a man but he was as tall as a tree and as silent and still as a statue. He wore a long black robe which stretched from his neck to his boney ankles. His face was as white as a sheet of paper and his eyes were two narrow slits. But what caught everyone's eye was a long bootlace moustache like a string of liquorice that swung all the way to his shoulders. Oh — and I nearly forgot. He was quite bald.

The narrow eyes blinked and instinctively Gus bowed. The others merely stared.

"You lish to speak?" He had a high monotonous voice.

"Great Mandarin," said Gus, bowing low. "We need your help if the Garden is not to be completely overruled by Thoth."

The Mandarin blinked — but said nothing.

"Will you help us?" Bilberry stared helplessly up at the inscrutable face, "Bracken has fallen into the Beneath World and we don't know how to get him back — or how to get rid of Thoth and those horrid Pines. We're in real trouble, Great Mandarin."

The Mandarin stared back at them all for a while, as though he was in some kind of trance. Then he raised a long thin hand and crooked one long thin finger at them.

"Tlubble in Garden?"

"Aye, awful trouble. Thoth is havin' a go at drivin' us all awee and makin' himself the Lord of the Place."

"Come with me." And the Mandarin clapped his hands together smartly. In ran a fat little Chinaman in soft black slippers with a long pigtail swinging halfway down his back.

"You lish to speak?"

"This Glate Assistan, Woo," said the Mandarin. He turned to Woo. "Make some tea for Honolable Guests." He bowed again and they all bowed back this time.

"Please sit." They all sat on the black and red cushions that lay scattered on the floor. The Mandarin, on the other hand, sat at the top of the room in a huge chair, black ebony, carved with hundreds of dragons and trees and fat smiling Buddhas and he pressed his fingers together.

When they had all had a drink out of the little porcelain dishes he spoke.

"What is Thoth up to?"

"He means to take over the Garden."

"Drive everything out."

"He marooned us on an island."

"He's already crushed I don't know how many bulbs."

"Most of the animals and birds have left already."

"He has sworn to make the Garden his and his alone and everyone else is to bend the knee to him."

"The Pines are a great army of bullies."

"Led by Captain Needle."

The Mandarin let them all speak until they had finished then he clapped his hands together smartly. "Woo," he said when the fat little Chinaman ran in, "fetch me the Glate Book of Owls."

Woo staggered in half a minute later carrying a huge leather bound book, dusty from lack of use and as thick as the trunk of a tree. He put it down on the table.

And then a strange thing happened.

Woo blew the dust off the top of the book and it landed on the Mandarin's face in the shape of a grand piano which stretched from his ear to his nose. Charlie tried not to giggle — he looked so funny with the weird shaped black mark on his face. Woo bowed low. "Permit me, Master," he said and blew very hard in a quick puff. The dust flew off, still shaped like a grand piano and gathered in the air then just as suddenly dropped to the floor. They all stared in amazement and looked back at the Mandarin's face. It was as white and clean as a sheet of paper again and their respect for the fat little assistant grew.

Gus fingered the red leather cover and read the engraved gold lettering on the front. "Why is it called the Books of Owls?"

The Mandarin stared at him severely. "Why are you called Gus?"

The boy thought for a minute. "I don't know — I suppose Mum and Dad just happened to like the name."

The Mandarin said nothing but opened the book at the first page. The paper was thick and as yellow as Jersey cream and on page one was a beautiful picture of a Tawny Owl sitting on the branch of a wide tree.

The Mandarin stroked the picture thoughtfully with one long skinny finger then he stared at each of the friends in turn — not forgetting the space where Macduff was sitting. He gave a tiny smile and began to talk.

"Many years ago," he said in his strange voice, "even before Glate Garden planted by Mr. Onoulable Bateman, when this countlee still Moorland, there live Glate Oak Tlee. In tlee live Wise Owl.

49

He know many things — how world leally made, how animals cleated by Gleat Good God — and he know much into future too. All things he know he lite in this book and call it Glate Book of Owls." He smiled again. "Now you know why it called that. In here.." He patted the book, "..he foretell future of Mr. Jame Bateman Garden."

"When Oak Tlee blown down by hunled mile an hour wind, Owl sleep with ancestors. Book then land in Honoulable lap. I am Keeper."

He bowed again and the four friends bowed back. But in the corner of the room, two yellow eyes blinked and a rustle of wind moved a little closer to peep at the book too.

CHAPTER 13

At last an answer

The Mandarin turned over page after page of the beautiful book and scanned the columns of writing. On some pages were lovely pictures of animals and plants, on others pictures of the big house which stood in the centre of the Gardens. There was a wide print of the Great Wall of China with all its turrets and on another page was a picture of a golden tree which radiated a warm glow. Before the Mandarin turned it over, Charlie read the caption underneath.

"Golden Larches," it said and the very picture gave her a warm, comfortable feeling.

But on the next page was a portrait of the Ape, great, huge black and hairy — looking every bit as ugly as when they had last seen him, eyes blazing like hot coals, teeth visible through a snarling mouth, squat head and hands like two great spades. Gus shuddered. In all the eleven years he had been alive he had never seen anything quite as repulsive as the Ape who lived in the tomb, guarded by the four stone sphinxes and with an army of Wellington Pines to do his bidding.

The Mandarin read out the words on the page facing, one long finger jabbing hard at the page, his brilliant jade ring flashing in the light as he moved his finger along the page. "And a day will come," he read, "when the Ape will attempt to become Lord of all the Garden and to drive out all species which will not obey him."

Underneath this caption, written in capital letters was this sentence. "THIS MUST NEVER HAPPEN".

The Mandarin's eyes narrowed to two black slits. "I think it is good thing you came to see me," he said.

50

"But how can we stop it?"

"I wonder if we ever can," Macduff said sadly.

"Of course we can." Gus felt angry. "We can't give up now. What would happen to Bracken and all the bulbs, the birds, the whole Garden. Mr. Bateman didn't plant it all just to be destroyed by Thoth."

The Mandarin nodded wisely and leafed over the page to another which had the heading "How to Defeat the Ape."

Underneath it read:

"The animals of the Garden cannot do this alone. They must enlist the help of the two human children, Gulliver and Charlotte Thornton."

Charlie looked at Gus with shining eyes. "It's us."

"The children can summon up the Golden Larches and thus defeat Thoth to return him once again to a stone statue who can do no harm. This is the way:

They must make their way to the Votive Dish at the bottom of the Bluebell Wood. Then they must place some small, personal thing into the bowl and summon up the Larches to their assistance with this rhyme:

"Golden Larches,
  standing tall,
Accept our Gift though it be small.
Help us defeat the Great Ape Thoth
And let Him feel Thy Golden Wrath.
Let rainbows shine down on our land
Watered by your gentle hand."

"Oh," said Charlie, "it's almost like a prayer to God."

Gus looked at her, "I suppose, in a way, it is."

"Hang on a minute." Gus put a finger at the very bottom of the page, "there's a P.S. here."

"What does it say?"

"Beware — for you have a traitor among you."

The yellow eyes blinked uncomfortably and faded while the friends looked at each other, dismayed.

CHAPTER 14

Back at the tomb of Thoth

"Lord Thoth," Cheese was saying in her slyest voice, "the Mandarin consulted the Book of Owls."

"That old rag?" the ape said scornfully, "what of it?"

"They're going to try and summon up the Golden Larches to help them," purred the cat.

"HA — let them try. Those larches haven't moved a root for years. I tell you, any life and powers they might once have had has gone." Thoth roared with laughter. "It should be fun watching a silly bush, an invisible piper and a couple of stupid children try and get a tree to help them defeat ME."

"But my Lord." The cat licked her lips nervously.

"You are dismissed," said the Ape. "Go and deal with the Universal Old Bag."

The cat didn't argue but slowly began to disappear, twitching tail first, sleek fat furry body, her ears and eyes and last of all her creamy, sly grin. She thought for a minute and decided that before dealing with the Universal Grandmother she would check on the children.

The four friends, led by Woo and the Mandarin were starting up the Bluebell Walk at the end of the Hundred Mile Way. Straight ahead of them, they could already see the huge stone votive dish at which they were to put their offerings.

"What are you going to put, Gus?"

"My watch," he said gloomily. "I'll miss it but... What are you going to put, Charlie?"

"My gold bracelet." She didn't need to say anymore.

As they walked up the path, tiny green shoots started pricking through the grass. The Mandarin smiled. "They are hopeful," he said and the Bluebells gave a thin cheer. "Hurray... hurray."

The massive stone dish felt surprisingly warm to their touch as though the stone had life of its own. Gus gave Charlie a leg up and she put the watch and the bracelet gently into the dish. Almost immediately a pink glow surrounded them and the two things were gone. Open-mouthed she watched until Gus groaned.

"Come on, Charlie, you're heavy."

"They've gone," she said, "disappeared." Behind them the Cheshire cat licked his lips nervously. He didn't like this one little bit.

Then Charlie and Gus linked hands with Bilberry and Macduff, the Mandarin and Woo and in loud, clear voices they marched around the votive dish and chanted.

"Golden Larches,
    Standing tall,
Accept our Gift though it be small.
Help us defeat the Great Ape Thoth
And let Him feel Thy Golden Wrath.
Let rainbows shine down on our land
Watered by your gentle hand."

A crash of thunder greeted their last words and they all fell to the ground, frightened. When they looked up, two silver swords lay shining on the grass. On the handle of one was engraved a small watch — on the handle of the other a picture of a bracelet. The Mandarin picked them up. "This is good," he said, "offeling accepted by Larches." And he nodded vigorously until the long bootlace moustache swung to and fro.

Their attention was diverted by a small robin with a fiery red breast swooping down towards them. "Thank Goodness I've found you," he said. "They're lined up. The bugle is about to sound."

Charlie felt sick. "But the Larches," she wailed.

Macduff spoke up. "We canna wait for them trees," he said. "I never really believed in them anyhow."

The Mandarin frowned but Gus picked up the sword and whirled it high above his head, suddenly feeling brave.

"Larches or no Larches," he said, "I've a score to settle with the Monkey. I'm not afraid of him, are you?"

"Never. I have ma Claymore..."

"And I my sword."

"And I have my sharp little twigs," Bilberry's voice squeaked nervously.

"Tune up your bagpipes, Macduff."

The Scotsman drew in a sharp breath and the next thing they heard was *"Scotland the Brave."*

"Come on, men....."

CHAPTER 15

The Battle and its Outcome

The Pines were crowded on one side of the Round Lawn. As soon as the friends marched around the side of the big house, they began to jeer.

"Now listen here," Macduff said when he had recovered his breath from the bagpipe playing, "let them see you mean business. Brandish your sword high above your head. Chop at their lower trunk and roots. Don't waste your energy on their branches. Get the roots, man."

"My family were all warring men and we Macduff's don't go into battle to lose. We go to win."

"I thought the Larches would help us," wailed Charlie.

"Mebbe they will but we still have to do all we can for ourselves."

Bilberry spoke up. "They don't look very life-like." They all glanced at the huge golden trees that sat motionless on the very edge of the lawn.

"Now you're not worryin' are ye, Lass?"

Bilberry waved her branches around. "When I think of Bracken," she said sadly, "I would fight anything to get him back."

Gus looked around at the friend's faces. "If we don't win....." He began again. "If anything happens, the only safe place I can think of is the Cheshire Cottage. The Universal Grandmother is safe from Thoth's magic. Go there if it looks as though we're losing the battle."

If he could have seen inside the Cheshire Cottage he would hardly have called it a safe place.

The cat had slunk away from the votive dish when the swords had appeared. Naturally cowardly by nature she had not liked the look of those sharp implements.

The Universal Grandmother had been busy polishing the windows when she had crept up behind her. She stretched out a claw. "I'll scratch her eyes out," she thought......

The friends were still standing facing the Pines when a cheering rose up from the back ranks. They were clustering around something huge and black that clanked in heavy metal armour. Slowly it moved forward to the sound of cheering that got steadily louder and louder.

The Mandarin stood calmly by and watched. "It is Thoth. They have brought him from the tomb. Once blood of any of us touches him he will be indestructable." From the sleeves of his silk robe, he produced a gleaming knife. "I too will fight."

"And I, Master." Woo jumped forwards, grinning. "I also Honouable Kalate Expert. Hi Hup!" and he chopped at the air with the sides of his hands.

"Excuse me," It was Monkey Puzzle, looking exactly as he had when they had last seen him. "Would you chaps mind awfully if I joined you?"

"Not at all, Laddie."

"They'll kill you all." Weeping Holly had left the Lakeside and was sidling up to them. "You haven't got a chance against all those Pines and Thoth. I shan't have any friends left if they kill you all. I shall be so lonely."

"Holly." Macduff spoke gently to the tree. "If we dinna fight they'll defeat us anyway and more than likely they'll torture us and kill us. At least this way we have a chance — even if it isn't a very good one," he added.

From the line of Pines, led by the clanking black figure, blasted a bugle. The Pines cheered loudly. "Thoth...Thoth...Thoth." and they swept in a low bow as Thoth moved forwards. The friends were frightened now.

A voice led them from the front. "Och we are not afraid of trees led by a monkey. "Come on, men."

Thoth gave a roar of fury and swished his sword through the air. But he couldn't see Macduff and Macduff gave him a blow on the neck. The trees rushed forwards, shouting and waving their branches in the air. But they couldn't see Macduff either and from the shouts of "Ouch!" and "Help!" he scored a good few blows.

Gus and Charlie moved into the thick of things, their silver swords held high above their heads. "Chop at their roots," shouted Gus and they soon got into the swing of things. (You see, once the trees roots were hacked away, they merely fell over like piles of firewood).

Thoth stood up, recovered from Macduff's blow and the Pines rallied round him, cheering loudly and waving their branches in the air.

Charlie looked around, dismayed. "We haven't got a chance," she said suddenly. "Look how many there are of them!"

Reinforcements were arriving all the time. To the left a small group of trees led by the battle scarred green Pine was marching towards them, chanting the old song — "Left Root Right Root...."

Gus looked over to the marching trees and was tempted to give up. The whole thing looked impossible.

Now for a moment we will leave the battle scene on the Round Lawn and return to the Cheshire Cottage where the Universal Grandmother had turned around to see Cheese licking her lips and staring at her with a quite unmistakable evil intent. For a while she stared at her then she spoke. "And I never even suspected you, Cheese," she said sadly. "I thought you were loyal to me."

55

The cat grinned. "I fooled you, didn't I, you silly old Moo. All the time I told everything straight to Thoth, my real master. You wouldn't believe all the things I was able to tell Him. He was grateful." Cheese licked her lips greedily. "He fed me on cream and best quality mice — not crummy old stew every day. He pampered me."

The Universal Grandmother shook her head sadly. "Pampering has its price, you know, Cheese. Thoth will get rid of you when he no longer needs you. You can't trust him."

The cat ignored her and shot out her claws. "I'll be the judge of that.

. . . .

And now — back to the battle scene. Gus was holding off two enormous Pines at the same time, trying to get at their roots with his silver sword. But each time he did, the other would whack him with his branches so he couldn't get a good swing at it.

Monkey Puzzle was valiantly swiping a few more Pines with his spikey branches, giggling as he did so "Take that, you overgrown weed," and "Here you are, you apology for a plant....."

And Macduff? Well, it's never easy to say exactly what Macduff is up to but judging from the sounds of a stout Scottish claymore chopping through soft roots, he was having an effect.

But Thoth's magic was powerful. He lifted the black visor and roared. And at the sound everyone stopped. The friends began to doubt and the Pines moved in for the kill.

CHAPTER 16

The Golden Larches

No one knew quite how the next thing happened but thinking hard about it later, Gus thought he remembered a sunbeam bouncing off the blade of his sword and reflecting on the two golden trees that stood at the side of the lawn.

What they all agreed on, talking about it later, was that the trees seemed to glow from inside the trunk with a golden blush — almost as though, Bilberry commented later, they had swallowed the sun. Then they grew quite hot with brilliance and the glow became white hot so even Thoth was forced to squeeze his eyes tightly shut. At the same time the Pines shrank to a little less than normal size and their roots slowly began to shrivel. Their leaves dulled and their branches stilled and the eye in the centre of the trunk disappeared quite suddenly with a quiet plop. The thin gash stuck with gooey resin and soon there was nothing left of the army but a long line of trees.

The Golden Larches next turned a white beam straight on Thoth and the friends watched, open-mouthed as he froze on the spot. The red eyes dulled. His fat hand dropped to his side and the sword clattered to the ground. In front of their very eyes his face became crumbling black stone and his armour cracked from bottom to top leaving nothing but granite. The ape they had all been so frightened of was nothing but a statue.

It was Bilberry who found her voice first. "They came," she said. "They did come. The larches helped us after all. Oh, I wish Bracken was here."

The Larches beamed down a concentrated golden light on the exact centre of the Round Lawn and the friends gathered round to watch. The light burned into the grass and a hole appeared, deep and black with steps up the side.

"Beneath World," the Mandarin whispered. "I had heard entlance was here, underneath Lound Lawn." And to their huge joy, up the steps, slowly hopped the frog, blinking at the unaccustomed light as he came.

Bilberry gave a shriek. "Bracken," she said, "and you're not even stone anymore. You're real." And she danced around and around the frog, laughing and crying at the same time.

Everyone had completely forgotten about Macduff. Of course, it was easy to do. He couldn't be seen. But the Larches hadn't forgotten. A white beam of light landed slightly off the centre and to everyone's astonishment, a man stood there, tall with fiery red hair and stocky legs which stuck out of a short tartan kilt. In one hand

57

were a set of bagpipes; in the other hand a short fat sword. They all stared at him. Gus was the first to speak. "Who on earth are you?"

"Do you not recognize me?" asked the strange man.

"You're voice is familiar."

"It's Macduff!"

Overhead was a loud sudden twittering of birds.

"The Swallows are back..."

And from underneath came an excited rumble and beneath their feet, sharp green shoots pricked through the grass. The bulbs had waited long enough for spring. They were impatient to get on.

Back in the Cheshire Cottage a white bundle was struggling in the corner, miaowing furiously and (I hate to say it), spitting.

You see, the Cheshire cat had reckoned without Universal Grandmother's damp sponge with which she had been cleaning the windows. She had flung it right into Cheese's face, blinding her for a minute. And a minute was just long enough. She whipped off her apron, wrapped the cat up inside it and pulled the strings round twice before knotting them — tightly.

Then she stopped and grinned. "Take that, you rotten traitor," she said.

CHAPTER 17
The Real Beginning

The rest of this story you can see for yourselves, if you visit Mr. Bateman's Garden. Thoth really was defeated and these days is nothing but a harmless black statue — although he still gives people quite a shock, stuck at the end of the long, black tunnel in the Egyptian Tomb, glaring at all the visitors.

Now the Pines stand perfectly obedient in a long line, outside the Cheshire Cottage where the Universal Grandmother keeps an eye on them.

Bracken had his wish and these peaceful days is a very happy real frog who swims in the lake all day long, catching flies and sunning himself on the island. But as a mark of respect a statue has been erected in the Gardens. See if you can find it.

Clue: The Red Ox challenges all who try to enter the Willow Pattern Garden.

The Mandarin still lives in the Joss House but you'll be very lucky indeed to see him or Woo. They keep themselves very much to themselves.

You might just catch sight of Bilberry though, scuttling around the Gardens, always worrying about something or other.

And Weeping Holly hasn't altered much either. She still spends at least half of her time, crying about something.

You definitely won't see Macduff. He left the Gardens, soon after the Battle of the Round Lawn and returned to his beloved Scotland, his bagpipes and Claymore tucked underneath his arm. The last I heard of him he was three quarters of the way up the M6.

Which brings us to Gus and Charlie. And here I have an Idea. Why don't you pretend you are them. Fight their battles, talk to all their friends in the Garden — or you could always have a game of Hide and Seek — that was how the whole thing started. Have a peep inside the Cheshire Cottage and see if you can spot the Universal Grandmother or even Cheese. You might even be offered a bowl of stew.

I think, having read this story that you will be glad to know that the Gardens will never be neglected again. The National Trust have bought the Gardens and will make sure history does not repeat itself (You know what I mean.) They intend putting right all the damage Thoth and his army caused over the years. And they are mending the Great Wall of China.

So enjoy the Gardens — as you were meant to do. But take my advice. Don't go alone into the Tomb of Thoth. Who knows what might happen?

THE END